HEARTS OF THE WEST

A Cowboy's Heart

The One That Got Away

By Jennifer Lewis

1

"Why would anyone get on the back of a bull?" Tara Kent couldn't take her eyes off the cowboy being tossed around like a rag doll by a fearsome black beast. Their ringside seats at the bull riding event were close enough for them to flinch from the flying sweat—or blood—of the obviously insane men competing.

"They're all thrill-seeking adrenaline junkies, darling." Melody's leering half smile was just embarrassing. "Mad as hatters but oh so hot!"

"I prefer a man with brains," Tara insisted, trying to convince herself.

"And look how far that's got you!" Melody shoved her with a bony elbow.

"Hey!" Tara wanted to protest, but the cowboy in the ring suddenly parted ways with the bull, rolled, jumped up and ran toward them, the bull hot on his heels.

Tara shrieked as he vaulted over the fence in front of them and landed almost right in her lap. The bull's huge horns thunked hard against the metal arena fence, and Melody screamed.

"Pardon me, ladies." The cowboy rose to his feet and doffed his hat. How was his hat still on his head after that exit? "Sorry about the intrusion."

He glanced back at the ring where the wranglers now had the bull under control and were guiding it out of the ring. "Had to make a hasty exit."

"Uh, no problem." Tara brushed dust from her skirt where he'd crushed against her. He was at least six feet of solid muscle clad in well-worn denim and a leather vest to protect his ribs.

"Melody McClain." Melody shoved out her manicured hand and brandished a bold red smile. "So pleased to meet you."

"Jesse West." He nodded his head. "Pleased to meet you, too." He shook Melody's hand then turned to Tara, his arm extended.

Jesse West? She once knew a Jesse West. Couldn't be the same one, though.

She realized he was still waiting for her to shake his hand. She wrapped her fingers around his and managed a polite smile and…holy….something shot through her, starting with her hand and streaking right up her arm and clobbering her in the chest. "Pleased to uh…" Words failed her. Why was heat flooding her body?

"Her name is Tara. Tara Kent," Melody offered. "She appears to have lost her manners."

Her manners were probably somewhere down on the dusty floor. At least he'd finally let go of her hand, but now he was looking at her with warm chocolate brown eyes that did something very alarming to her insides.

"Tara." His eyes widened slightly. "Jesus, Tara. Is it you?"

She blinked. "Jesse." *Seriously, where was her brain?*

"Yes." He tipped his hat back slightly. His features

were stronger, bolder and more chiseled than they'd been all those years ago, but now that she had a chance to look at him... "It's been, what, ten years?"

"You two know each other?" Melody's question hovered somewhere outside them.

"Ten years. Yes." *Phew.* At least she could speak now. He was always good looking—in a raw boyish way—but the passage of years had been very, very kind to Jesse West. "You're taller."

A smile creased his tanned face. "Yep. And you're more beautiful than ever. Holy cow, Tara. We need to catch up. Can I take you ladies out for a drink? I'm done riding for now."

"Of course, we'd love to," cut in Melody, before Tara even had time to form words. Jesse ignored Melody and kept his eyes fixed right on hers.

"Uh, a drink. Sure. That would be great," she stammered. She didn't have to tell him the sad story of her broken engagement. She could just pretend like everything was great. A quick drink and—

How did sweet, gentle Jesse West become a big, burly rodeo cowboy?

"Darling, aren't you even going to look at your score?" Melody seized Jesse's arm. "What does ninety-one mean? Is that good?"

"It's just fine." He smiled warmly at them. "Let's go."

Jesse walked a few steps behind the two ladies as they headed out of the arena. Tara Wicklow! He'd spent ten long years wondering what happened to her. And now she showed up when he was in the fight of his life for the world championship title.

He couldn't miss this chance to reconnect. New

last name, though. She must be married.

On the plus side, if she was married, he could put her out of his mind for good.

"This way, ladies." They turned. Damn, she was even more beautiful than before. There was something fragile about her now, too, that tugged at his heart. "A friend of mine has a private enclosure set up where we can relax." They headed out of the arena and down a side hallway that led to the VIP areas.

Gorgeous body, too. He couldn't help but stare as she walked down the hall, hips swinging oh-so-slightly inside her slim skirt.

"Turn right here." He gestured for them to enter a small enclosure marked "Leader Whiskey," one of his sponsors. The enclosure had comfortable chairs for the company big wigs and a waiter smiled at them from behind the bar.

"We don't have to drink whiskey, do we, darling?" Tara's friend turned and lifted a penciled brow.

"Nah. They have water to mix it with. We can have some of that." He teased her with a wink.

Once the bartender had poured two glasses of white wine for the ladies and a stiff glass of seltzer for him—he never drank during a competition—they sat in the leather chairs and he leaned back and took in the delicious vision in front of him. Tara Wicklow—the one that got away.

"You're probably wondering what happened to me," she said, glancing up at him.

"Indeed I am. You disappeared right into thin air." And right after the momentous night when he'd finally gotten to kiss her.

"My family moved. I had to change schools." She

4

took a quick sip of her wine. "I'm sorry I didn't stay in touch."

He'd had to tough out his final year at that miserable waspy New England boarding school without his fellow Texan to commiserate with. And with the memory of that kiss on his lips. "I'm sorry, too. I looked for you a few times, over the years, but I never found a trace of you."

She shrugged and a fake laugh tinkled in the air. "I lived in New York for a couple of years. I came back to Texas when my mom got sick. She's better now, though."

"I'm glad to hear it. Are you married?" He couldn't hold out another minute before asking. Desire was building inside him along with a million questions and if he learned she was married he'd take a fire hose to it.

She swallowed, and looked back down at her wine glass. "No."

"Divorced?" *Uh-oh*. His question sounded just a little too perky.

She shook her head, lips pressed together.

"She's just had her heart ripped in two by a man who strung her along for six years." Melody shook her head.

Tara's eyes widened. "Melody! You said you wouldn't—"

"As Beyoncé says, "if you want it then you need to put a ring on it," isn't that right, Jesse?"

"Absolutely." He was warming to her friend.

"It's *should have* put a ring on it," protested Tara. "The lyrics. That's how they go."

"And that's what he should have done, the idiot." Melody sighed. "So finally Tara had the good sense to break up with him. And here we are!" She looked from Jesse to Tara and back again.

Sweet. Jesse fought to stop a grin from creeping across his mouth.

Melody smiled a mysterious smile. "Darling, can I smoke in here?"

"I don't think so." He couldn't take his eyes off Tara.

"Drat. I'm gasping for one. Tara's no help. She just quit."

"I'm glad to hear it." How did she get even more gorgeous? She still had those big watery blue eyes, and the soft blond hair. Her elegant figure was just a tiny bit fuller, so even more enticing. Damn. How many nights had he dreamed about pressing his body up against it? Lust roared through him and he fought to tamp it down.

"I'll just step outside by myself then. You don't mind, do you, Tara?"

Tara looked panicked and moved her feet as if she was about to rise to them.

Adrenaline roared through Jesse. He'd missed her for ten long years. There was no way he could let her slip away now. "We'll wait right here for you. We have a lot to catch up on."

2

Tara sipped her wine cautiously. She didn't want to take even the slightest chance of getting tipsy. Not around Jesse. Not when he looked this tall and ripped and gorgeous and quite unlike any other man she'd ever met. The conversation would be safer if she seized the reins. "How did you become a cowboy?"

"I did grow up on a ranch." A smile tugged at the corners of his mouth. "At least before my family shipped me up to our snooty school in New Hampshire in a failed attempt to turn me into American aristocracy."

"The school wasn't so bad." She'd been devastated when her parents had informed her they couldn't afford her senior year there.

"For me it was hell. People made fun of me from the moment I showed up. They used to call me Longhorn for reasons I don't even know."

"They teased me for being from Texas, too, but that's just ignorance. Those New Englanders don't know what they're missing. They think Texas is all desert and cows and people with huge hats." She glanced at his big cowboy hat.

"You were popular. Everyone loved you. I was so honored that you took the time to be friends with me." He said it softly, and it was a funny confession coming out of such a big, tough cowboy.

She'd felt sorry for him. He was kind and shy and totally a fish out of water among all the preppy kids from Connecticut. "It was nice to be able to talk to someone from back home and not worry about being teased for my accent," which she'd worked hard to get rid of, "or asked why I didn't wear cowgirl boots."

"I had a huge crush on you. Did you know that?"

"I realized it at the end, when we…." She hadn't thought about that kiss in years. It had blown her away at the time. It was the last night before the long summer vacation and she was spilling all her problems, all her sadness about her parents' divorce, to sweet, kind Jesse and then—vooom!

"Kissed. I've never forgotten that kiss." His dark eyes crinkled into a wistful smile. "I was devastated when you didn't come back after the summer. When you didn't stay in touch at all."

She sighed. She'd felt bad about that too, but she just couldn't bear for her former schoolmates to know what had really happened. She wanted them to remember her as glamorous and fun and… She didn't want them to know that her father had lost everything and that her parents were splitting up. "It was worse than I told you." She frowned. Did she really need to tell him?

"You said your parents were separating." His dark eyes shone with understanding that threatened to make her spill all. She steeled herself to keep to the barest facts. No one really knew the truth except her immediate family and she planned to keep it that way.

"Yes. They got divorced that summer." Her dad had cheated on her mom and they all learned he'd been doing it for years. "And there was no money for me to finish school." None of her blue blood classmates had known that her dad wasn't a bond broker or a CEO like theirs. He was a professional gambler. In one big, foolish gamble he'd lost everything, including their house in Austin. His secret mistress had turned up on their doorstep when he stopped making her car payments. Her whole life had exploded that year.

"I figured it was something like that. I tried looking you up online, but there was no trace of you."

"I changed my name to my mom's maiden name. It sounds crazy but I was so mad at my dad. I felt like he'd betrayed us all." She swallowed. How had she let the conversation stray in this direction? "And you still haven't explained how you became a rodeo cowboy."

"My mom always blamed my brother Bowie. He's a year younger than me but was always a big daredevil. He started riding bulls and got me to give it a try, and soon I was hooked. He's competing here, too. He's kicking himself for getting me started because now I'm higher in the rankings than he is."

"And it pays a real living?"

"It does now. In the beginning I admit I was living off my inheritance for a while there."

Inheritance? Jesse had never talked about having money. But then he wouldn't, would he? He was always modest and shy to a fault. He'd hardly have been at the Andover Academy if his parents were piss-poor rednecks.

"If I win the championship tomorrow, there's a million dollar prize."

"Are you going to win?"

"It's a very real possibility. The ride you just saw

kept me in the number one spot."

"Wow. That's great." She tried to keep a bright smile on her face. She was hustling to find her rent and he had an "inheritance" and a million dollars coming his way. "You must be very talented."

"You did just see me in action." That slow smile crept across his face. "And that bull is the meanest one here this year. I was lucky to draw it."

"Lucky?"

"You only get a high score if the ride is difficult. The last thing a bull rider wants is a quiet bull that will just skip around the arena. We want a fire-breathing, rip snorting monster." His grin revealed sparkling white teeth.

Damn. Why was he so cute? She didn't remember him being this adorable as well as ridiculously handsome. He must have women following him everywhere. She couldn't resist asking, "Are you married?"

"Would you marry someone crazy enough to do this for a living?" he teased.

"No way." It was a relief to have a chance to reject him, even as a joke.

"And I guess I just never met the right woman." His gaze rested on hers for a moment. *Not after you.* Tara imagined him saying that—almost heard the words in her head—then quickly dismissed them. She must have a really big ego! It was amazing he even remembered her after all these years.

"I'm glad you recognized me," she said brightly. "I guess it's good that I don't look too different after so much time."

"You're prettier than ever. I'd recognize those eyes anywhere. I don't think I've ever seen anyone with that same exact shade of blue."

"People sometimes ask if I'm wearing contacts. I do color my hair these days, though. Now that I'm inside all day it doesn't get a chance to turn pale blonde in the summer any more." Why had she said that? She felt a strange urge to be humble around Jesse. She'd felt sorry for him back then, and now here he was, a big rodeo star and she was...

Her heart squeezed.

"What do you do inside all day?"

She shrugged. "Decorating people's houses. Picking wall colors, choosing pictures and arranging furniture. Nothing too exciting."

He cocked his head to the side. "You always wanted to own your own business."

She cringed to think of the big plans she must have shared with him back then. She always thought she'd be CEO of a big corporation by now. "I do, really. I work for myself." She heard a lame tinkling laugh emerge from her throat. "I'm trying to grow my designs into a brand. That's my big plan, anyway. Melody and I are here in Vegas to hopefully decorate a Tuscan-style mansion out in the hills. My client is a huge rodeo fan so he gave us the tickets for today. He's in there somewhere, milling around."

The job wasn't in the bag yet, and it was BIG one. It would support her for at least a year, maybe even two if she nailed it. And from what she'd seen of the house it would make an amazing magazine spread that would really get her name out there.

She wondered if Jesse would agree to meet her client. An introduction to the top bull rider could clinch the deal. She didn't want to ask a big favor of Jesse right now though. Not after they'd just met.

"Would you have dinner with me tonight?"

His question caught her off guard. "Uh, I'm here with Melody, and we—"

"I'll bring my brother Bowie. He's here competing, too. The four of us could go out together."

Melody's voice rang out from behind her back. "What a marvelous idea, darling! I do hope Bowie is as rugged and charming as you."

Tara cringed slightly. Melody was way too blunt. And she didn't really want to spend more time with Jesse. He was too handsome and reminded her of a time when she thought she had the world at her feet—she'd planned to apply to an Ivy league school!—that truly felt like another lifetime.

"Tara?" Jesse didn't take Melody's answer as her own. That was sweet of him.

"Sure. Why not?" She hoped she didn't sound as wary as she felt. And if his brother was half as good looking as him, Melody would be pawing him and trying to get an invitation to his hotel room. "Where should we meet?"

"We'll pick you ladies up at your hotel. Where are you staying?"

Thankfully their client was being billed to put them up somewhere fancy—all part of selling yourself as "the best"—so she gave him the address without hesitation. Then he walked them back to the stands.

"I'm in heaven, darling." Melody stared at all the cowboys milling around.

"Can we go?" Tara's nerves were getting frayed by all the noise and crowds. And watching young men getting tossed around by bulls wasn't exactly relaxing. "I think we've spend enough time here to tell Gareth how amazing it was. We should go back to the hotel and work on our sketches."

Melody let out a big sigh and tossed her chestnut hair. "You're such a party pooper. But I guess it will give me time to primp for tonight."

"Behave yourself tonight, lady. I was thinking we could ask the brothers if they'll meet Gareth and maybe have a drink with him. Don't you think he'd love that?"

"You're a genius. He'd be purple with excitement."

"We can ask later. So we need to stay on their good side."

"And if that involves going back to their rooms for a nightcap, I'll do my best to oblige." Melody waggled her penciled eyebrows.

"What if his brother looks like one of the bulls?"

Melody laughed. "I'll take my chances. I like 'em burly and a little rough around the edges."

They went back to their double room and Tara started putting together a digital collage of her ideas. Melody got a facial in the hotel spa and took a nap. She was possibly the world's worst assistant— especially since she insisted on being called a "Vice President"—but she was amazing at bringing in new clients. Also, she agreed to work for a percentage of the profits and didn't have to be paid up front.

And right now, freshly alone and feeling vulnerable, Tara needed all the emotional and actual support she could get.

She wore a simple blue sheath dress that brought out the color in her eyes. Was there any shame in wanting to look good? It was nice to be admired, especially when you were still wading your way out of the wreckage of a broken relationship.

Melody put on a ridiculous getup with high-heeled

cowgirl boots, ultra tight black jeans and a low cut shirt. She looked up from penciling on her eyeliner at the mirror. "I guess if they're sharing a room, too, one of us can go to their room and the other can come back here."

"Why?"

"To have sex, of course! Why else?"

"I'm not having sex with anyone."

"Ever again?" Melody's slim brow lifted.

"Possibly not, but it's too soon to commit. I'm certainly not having sex with anyone tonight."

"But darling, an erotic fling is just what you need. It'll help you rebound properly."

"I went to high school with him, for crying out loud." She certainly wasn't going to mention that she'd kissed him.

"All the better. You can skip over all the getting-to-know-you bullshit and get right down to business." She stuck a hand in her purse and pulled out a tin. "Here, have a breath mint."

"I don't need a breath mint. I'm not kissing anyone, either."

A sneaky smile tugged at the corners of Melody's painted mouth. "We'll see."

3

"Oh. My. God." Melody's dramatic tones made Tara look up from her phone. It seemed like every head in the hotel lobby swiveled toward the revolving door where two tall cowboys just made an entrance.

"I guess he doesn't look like a bull." Tara tried to distract her attention from Jesse's lean, muscular form by focusing on his brother Bowie. A tall drink of whiskey in a pale straw cowboy hat, with a powerful build evident under his faded jeans and pale blue shirt. Jesse wore a black hat tonight, and dark clothing—a black shirt and dark denim—that gave him an air of mystery.

"He's unbelievable, darling. Look at those shoulders."

"Stop staring, you'll scare him," she whispered.

"I don't think anything could scare this cowboy." Tara watched a big goofy smile spread across Melody's face as she started across the lobby toward him.

Jesse made the introductions and Bowie gallantly flirted with Melody as they walked to a restaurant where he'd made reservations. Tara tried to ignore the awareness that pricked her every time she looked at Jesse. He was a cowboy, for crying out loud! He wouldn't be the slightest bit interested in her, a woman who's idea of an outdoor activity was shopping for shoes.

Still, he was unbelievably handsome. He led them into a restaurant with white tablecloths, which rather surprised her. For some reasons she'd anticipated a rib joint.

And he pulled out her chair like a perfect gentleman. She fought the urge to purr like a contented cat as she settled into it.

"So where do you boys stay when you're in town?"

"The Mandarin Oriental, usually," said Bowie. "Jesse likes it because it's quiet."

Melody's eyes widened. "That's a five star hotel. You must be making some serious money clinging to the back of those beasts."

Bowie laughed. "Enough to pay for a good night's sleep, anyway."

Tara decided not to mention that they were independently wealthy with inherited money. It wasn't any of her business to start with, and it would turn Melody into a monster. She thought men were good for two things, sex and money—both at the same time was an ideal, though rare, arrangement.

"I think it's great that you make a living doing what you love," she ventured. "That's why I got into design."

"Do you have to travel for work all the time, too?" asked Jesse. Damn those soft brown eyes.

"Not that often." She'd never even considered traveling when she was with Gordon. She'd put her career on the back burner to be the perfect girlfriend, cooking gourmet meals at his house and always available for glittering charity events. "This trip is unusual for me. There's enough work around Austin to keep an army of decorators busy these days."

"I'll bet." His smile crinkled the corners of his eyes. "All the travelling is my least favorite part of this gig. I'm really hoping to win tomorrow so I can retire and plough the winnings into a piece of land I own outside Austin."

"What would you do there?"

"Train and sell horses."

"And breed bucking bulls," cut in Bowie.

"You can breed the bucking bulls. I'll focus on the horses."

"I'm nowhere near retiring yet," said Bowie with a grin. "I'm not ready to settle down. So I won't be there in the morning to feed the bulls."

"Maybe we can come to an arrangement," said Jesse, with a slow grin. "If I win tomorrow, that is."

"Are you two in direct competition against each other?" asked Tara.

"Yep." Jesse glanced at Bowie. "But tomorrow night he's going to get the butt whoopin' of a lifetime."

"In your dreams, bro." Bowie's jade green eyes sparkled with amusement.

"You're both very relaxed about this. Some people would be figuring out how to slip poison into the other's drink." Their lack of hostility was totally charming.

"We've been at this since childhood. Bowie dragged me into the rodeo circuit because it was too boring without some real competition, right Bowie?"

"Exactly. And I'd have had to share my hotel room with some smelly guy who'd leave his socks on the radiator. Better to keep it in the family."

"What are you going to do when Jesse retires?" asked Melody, her eyes bright with lust.

"He won't retire. Because I'm going to win tomorrow."

Jesse lifted a brow. "Maybe I should just poison him."

"I don't think so, darling. I have plans for him." She shone a bright smile on Bowie, who was kind enough to smile back. Or was he really going to sleep with her? Tara didn't know exactly how old Melody was—such things were utterly off limits—but she was at least ten years older than Bowie. Possibly closer to twenty if she'd had as much plastic surgery as she insinuated.

After dinner they went to a club with a rooftop garden. The Vegas heat had been intense in the daytime, but now it was cool and pleasant. A band played upbeat country music and they enjoyed a view over the twinkling lights of Vegas, and the dark, empty desert in the distance.

"Thank goodness we're outdoors. I'm dying for a smoke." Melody tapped out one of her long Sobranies.

"That's why I chose it." Jesse said softly. "And I'm also hoping for a dance."

"Uh…" He had just paid for dinner, but she had no idea how to dance to country music, and was rusty at any kind of dancing. Gordon would rather die than get up on a dance floor.

"I might cry if you say no." The way his eyes sparkled he looked more likely to laugh than cry, but it made her smile.

"I suppose I'd better say yes, then. But I hope you're wearing protective footwear." She glanced down at his sturdy cowboy boots.

"Won't be any worse than a horse stepping on my foot." He rose and offered her his hand. He'd left his hat on the table and his hair was slicked back slightly to reveal the bold cut of his features. He looked like he'd just stepped out of a magazine fashion spread on the old West. Most women would be salivating to take his hand.

She just felt nervous. Her ego was battered by Gordon dating her for six years then—when she gave him an ultimatum that they needed to get engaged now or never—he'd told her he wasn't ready for a serious commitment.

And she'd had no choice but to make good on her threat and break up with him. Which sucked, because she still had feelings for him. Or maybe she'd just invested so much energy in him, and in planning their future together, that it was like walking away from a company you'd worked hard to build.

Onward and upward! She took Jesse's hand and the heat that immediately spread to her palm alarmed her. There was definitely some kind of chemistry crackling between them and she didn't like it.

She was too vulnerable right now to get sucked into something, then chewed up and spat out again. She'd be a lot safer back in her hotel room looking at curtain swatches online.

Her eyes widened as he slid his arm around her waist. She sucked in a breath and tried to stay calm. *Just dance with him, be nice, then wish him good night.* She could do this.

She tried to remind herself that this was her old friend Jesse, the sweet boy an inch shorter than her who she used to reminisce about blistering Austin summer days with when they were both freezing their butts off in a New England winter.

It didn't work.

This Jesse was a whole different animal. His once skinny body was now ripped with muscle, no doubt gained from jumping on and off horses and bulls and heaving big saddles around. Formerly shy, he now oozed quiet confidence that disarmed her.

His other arm circled her and he held her close and swayed gently in time to the music. His subtle masculine scent crept over her senses and she blinked, trying to halt the effect it had on her. She could feel her pulse rate accelerate and her breathing grow shallow. Her skin grew hotter by the second and she could barely stay upright on her feet because her knees were getting weak…

"Are you okay?" He pulled her a little closer.

Her breasts weren't quite touching his chest yet— they weren't that big—but any minute now her nipples were going to brush up against the crisp fabric of his shirt and—"I am feeling a little light headed."

"Don't worry. I'll catch you if you pass out." His slow smile crept across his mouth—a wide, sensual mouth with perfectly shaped lips that she didn't remember at all—and further unraveled her.

She attempted to move her hips to the music but with no natural sense of rhythm, it wasn't easy. She just felt more awkward and clueless and foolish by the minute. Here she was drooling over him like a teenager and he was cool and relaxed as could be.

Boy, how the tables had turned.

Her mind and body were now at war. Her treacherous torso sizzled in his arms and heat roamed through her like steam. Her mind was begging her to flee—plead a headache, indigestion, even a trip to the bathroom!

Thankfully, just when she was about to burst into flames of desire and embarrassment, the song ended. "Let's sit down," she begged, way too fast.

He must have heard the panic in her voice. "Sure, let's go sit where we can see the view." He said it with the same easy charm he'd displayed all night. Did nothing get this man rattled? No doubt you needed nerves of steel to climb on top of a bull. She wasn't made of such stern stuff.

He led her over to a sort of sofa that looked out over the Vegas lights below. Tara glanced back at the table where Melody and Bowie were leaning together, laughing. Maybe they wanted to be left alone.

She sat on the sofa and braced herself as Jesse eased his big, muscled body into position beside her. It's a shame she didn't smoke any more. It would have kept her hands busy and blowing smoke would have kept him at a distance.

"I get the feeling I'm making you tense." His dark eyes shone with curiosity—and if she wasn't mistaken, a hint of amusement.

Tara swallowed. "Nonsense. I'm fine. Just worried about the big commission I'm here for." She certainly didn't want him to know that close physical proximity to him was gradually unhinging her. "That probably seems funny to you when you have the biggest bull ride of the year tomorrow."

"I just take it in my stride. Fretting doesn't make me perform better. Tell me about your commission. What would you be doing?" He looked genuinely interested.

"It's a new house, just built, so we need to choose

the flooring and cabinetry before we even get started. Then the usual stuff—choosing wall colors that work with the prevailing light, window treatments, furnishings and accessories. It's also nearly eleven thousand square feet so there's a lot of space to decorate. It would be my biggest commission ever, if I get it."

"Sweet."

Now was a good time to ask if he'd meet her client. But did she really want to owe him a favor?

Twelve to twenty four months of solid work plus the possibility of placement in prestigious architectural magazines versus…applying for a sales assistant position at Pottery Barn. Since she' d moved out of Gordon's house her expenses had shot up and her usual small commissions weren't enough to support her. "My client is a big rodeo fan."

His face brightened. "No kidding. If there's anything I can do to help you clinch the deal, let me know."

"Well, I was wondering, maybe you could say hello to him at the finals tomorrow, or something. He'll be there."

"I'd be delighted. Maybe he could be one of my guests at the after party. Along with you and Melody, of course."

"Are you serious?" Gareth would be beside himself if he got an invitation to the VIP after party. He was a very sweet and humble guy who'd made a fortune manufacturing plastic lunch trays. He'd recently sold his company and moved to Vegas from Omaha. From what she'd gathered he had loads of money but still felt like an outsider. "He'd be over the moon."

"Consider it done. Just bring him on over tomorrow night and I'd be glad to show him around and introduce him to some folks." Then he cocked his head. "On one condition."

"What?" Her heart was fluttering with the excitement of nailing this commission. She could already picture herself proudly bragging about it back in Austin. Even Gordon might be slightly impressed.

"That you give me another kiss."

4

Tara blinked. "*Another* kiss?" She hadn't kissed him at all. Not even hello. She'd have remembered.

"I'm counting our first kiss, behind the swimming pool building."

"That was—" A long time ago. A kiss? "This sounds like bribery to me. Isn't that illegal?"

She snuck a glance at his mouth. It was a very sensual mouth. The kind of mouth that it might be very hard to stop kissing, once you made the mistake of starting. And it definitely would be a mistake.

"I'm not familiar with the laws here in Nevada, but since they have brothels and legal gambling I don't think they're going to get too hot under the collar about my suggestion." His eyes sparkled with amusement. "And I've been thinking about kissing you all night."

His words caused the flame of heat he'd been stoking to flare inside her. She tried to ignore it. He hadn't tried to kiss her at all tonight. She'd think someone as confident and gorgeous as Jesse would just go in for the kill. But no doubt she was sending out all kinds of prickly get-away-from-me signals. This was his way of politely asking.

If she refused to kiss him, she'd be making a big

deal over nothing and now it would be really awkward to try to bring Gareth to the after party. One kiss really wasn't much, was it? Just one kiss.

"I don't suppose one kiss in exchange for a favor could be considered prostitution, could it?"

"Definitely not. But even if it was, we are in Nevada." His pupils darkened. She could read the desire in his eyes. "I think you should risk it."

"I'll bet you do." His obvious interest excited her. Right now she felt downright desirable—something she hadn't experienced in a long time. Her dented confidence swelled and started to preen itself. "But then you're obviously more of a risk taker than me. I don't ride bulls."

"Not yet, anyway." He winked, and the slow smile spreading across his mouth blew more heat on the blaze inside her. "You never know what could happen once you start living dangerously."

"That's what I'm worried about." A smile snuck across her mouth, too, and she couldn't stop it. Jesse amused and tempted her at the same time.

He leaned in a little, until their faces hovered about six inches apart. Her lips twitched, moving involuntarily. *You're going to kiss him.* Her heart beat so hard he could probably hear it. She watched his face grow closer, until she could see the five-o-clock shadow on his chiseled cheek, then her eyes slid closed, and their lips met in a rush.

Heat stormed through her. His scent was intoxicating—leather and horses and strong, hard male. The kiss started out soft, their lips touching and exploring each other, then she felt his arms ease around her waist, drawing her into a warm embrace.

Electricity sparked inside her as the tips of their

tongues met. Her arms flew around him—she needed to steady herself—and she drew in the delicious smell of him as her tongue danced with his. Her nipples sizzled inside her shirt and the fire below her belly was in danger of jumping out of bounds and burning down the whole state of Nevada.

How did this man have such an effect on her?

Because he was gorgeous, charming, funny, sweet…and Jesse.

When they finally pulled apart she was sweating and gasping like she'd just run a mile. She blinked—the outdoor lanterns seemed painfully bright—and tried to look anywhere but at him. "I hope that was okay," she stammered, trying to make light of the most intense and insane kiss of her whole life.

"It was a heck of a lot more than okay, and I'm pretty sure you know that." His dark eyes blazed. "It was worth every single day of the ten years I waited to enjoy it."

Her lips still sizzled with awareness of his. "Is it really ten years?"

"We were sixteen." He looked at her mouth, and her lips parted involuntarily. "Or I was. I think you were seventeen. I remember you had a few months on me." A cute dimple showed when he smiled.

"Thanks for reminding me that I'm older than you. I probably thought that made me cooler back then. Now I'm not so sure." A smile crept over her mouth again. Jesse was so easy to tease and talk to. But then he always had been.

They'd soon run out of things to say, though. They had nothing in common except for the fact that they'd both attended Andover Academy. Big difference—he'd graduated from Andover and she got her diploma from a big public high school. She was still bitter about that. One lousy year there and it was the educational institution noted on her resumé for the rest of her life.

She was trying her best to distract herself from the odd fluttering in her chest, but it wasn't working. "You're so much taller than I remember."

"I grew five inches between senior year and the end of college. We're late bloomers in my family. You're more beautiful than ever."

She laugh-snorted. Then blushed. Eek! What kind of effect was he having on her? "Wow, I'm so good at taking a compliment. Mostly because I don't believe it." She'd gained a few pounds since the big break-up with Gordon last month and was self-conscious about it.

"I don't understand why your ex-boyfriend wasn't rushing to marry you."

"Me either." She laughed. Not that it was funny. "I kept thinking he was just about to propose. We even lived together, but after six years I decided I'd better give him an ultimatum." Should she really tell him this? Why not. It's not like she was hoping to start dating him. The kiss was just part of a deal, right?

"An ultimatum?" Curiosity shone in his eyes.

"Either I see a ring by December 25th, or we part ways."

"That was cute. You gave him the idea of a Christmas proposal."

"Yeah, adorable, right? Anyway, he said that he didn't feel like he could make that kind of commitment so we'd better go our separate ways."

"Ouch. Who moved out?"

"Me. It was his house, unfortunately. It was

especially unfortunate that I had decorated the whole thing and it looked fabulous."

"And that was this year?" He looked surprised.

"Just last month. I stayed with Melody while I found myself a new apartment, and I only just finished moving my stuff in—while he was out at work—before we left for Vegas."

"Sounds like you needed a Vegas getaway."

"I guess you're right."

"They do say the best way to get over an old lover is to find a new one."

"Is that what men say? Because that sounds like a guy thing. Women generally recommend spending some quality time binge watching your favorite TV series and eating gourmet ice cream. Less likely to end in tears."

That irresistible smile still played about the corners of his mouth. Even as she told him her pathetic break-up sob story, he still looked at her like she was some kind of goddess. She had to admit it was good for her ego.

"I guess the guy strategy is more risky, but it's also more fun."

"You don't know how many shows I want to catch up on. Gordon always wanted to watch Law & Order. I think I've seen every episode ever made of that show. Which is about a million."

"I don't think I've seen it even once."

"I like that about you." That goofy smile was sneaking over her mouth again. "You are the exact polar opposite of Gordon Van Zant."

"Then I guess he was short, skinny, conservative and dull."

"He was six-four, but you're not too far off on the

other counts."

"Were you in love with him?" Jesse's eyes crinkled again. He was curious.

Her heart squeezed. The pain was still so fresh. Maybe that's why he asked. To find out if she was still in love with Gordon. "Of course. Why else would I want to marry him?"

"I guess it's pretty crude of me to force you to kiss me when you're still carrying a torch for another guy."

"You didn't force me. Besides, it's about time I shoved that torch into a pile of manure."

"I know where they pile the manure from all the bulls in the contest." He lifted a brow.

She burst out into a laugh. "I wish I could throw him in it."

"Don't waste your energy. I can think of better things for you to do with it."

And just like that they were kissing again. *Uh-oh.* Her mouth welcomed his and their tongues tangled. He held her tight enough for her to feel the cut of his muscles through his shirt, all that raw strength drawing them close.

Silver sparkles danced behind her eyelids. That was a first! Kissing Jesse was completely different than kissing any man she'd ever met. And she'd kissed a few in her time, before Gordon. None of them as breathtakingly handsome as this one, though.

His strong fingers pressed into her back, stirring sensation and crushing her nipples against his chest. It felt amazing. She let her fingers roam up into his thick hair and explore the roping muscles of his neck and shoulders.

This was so much more fun than kissing Gordon, even though she had no thoughts of a future with

Jesse. Maybe *because* she had no thoughts of a future with Jesse. She could enjoy this moment—and him—for exactly what they were right now. No worries about what hadn't happened yet or what needed to happen or what was or wasn't going to happen if she said the wrong thing.

She regretted her ultimatum. It was an act of ego that she'd have to live with for the rest of her life.

But kissing Jesse was a fabulous antidote to her sadness. So what if he was a crazy devil-may-care rodeo cowboy? That made him all the more perfect for a wild Vegas fling.

Their kiss had deepened and her whole body now pressed against his. Thank goodness they were hidden away in a dark area of the roof garden. His big denim-clad thighs pressed against hers and she enjoyed the power of his body.

She could sleep with him.

The idea made her brain freeze and her lips stopped moving.

"What's the matter?"

"I just realized I—" She scrambled for an excuse. "I forgot to make a phone call."

"Yeah, to your client so you can invite him to the VIP after party."

"That too." Crazy thoughts spun through her head. Or maybe her brain wasn't the body part responsible. This man had an alarming but very invigorating effect on her body.

What happens in Vegas, stays in Vegas, right? Even if there was no future between them, a night in Jesse West's bed might be a very good way to recover from the breakup hangover slump she'd been stuck in for weeks.

Or would she end up falling madly in love with him and being devastated when he moved on to a gorgeous cowgirl next week.

No. There was no way she could fall for a rodeo cowboy, or even a cowboy of the lives-on-a-ranch variety. She enjoyed a certain lifestyle—city living, parties, socializing—and that was not Jesse's scene at all. She suppressed a laugh at the thought of him wearing his big cowboy hat to a dance at Gordon's golf club. But it wouldn't be funny in real life.

"What's so funny?" He looked at her curiously.

"You. Me. This…" She waved her hand in the air. "What are we doing?"

"We're just having a friendly reunion." His lips hovered close, and her mouth tingled with awareness.

A friendly reunion? That was one way of putting it. Maybe this was how he greeted all his old female friends. Maybe he wouldn't even want to sleep with her.

Either way, she'd better get out of here before she did something she might live to regret. "Don't you need to get some sleep before your big ride tomorrow?"

"It's only 8 seconds long."

"But you need to be alert."

"I'm always alert, lady."

"I believe you. I need to get some sleep, though. I need my wits about me when I try to charm my client into spending vast amounts of money for my expertise."

"I hear you." He smiled slowly. "I'm looking forward to watching you in action."

"He really is going to be thrilled about meeting you."

"I already love the guy. He gave me a chance to kiss you." His eyes twinkled with amusement—and something else. Something more, that she couldn't put her finger on.

Which was fine, since her fingers had already been all over him.

"Let's not tell him about our deal, okay?"

5

Tara didn't want Jesse joking about their bargain. He was so laid back he might think it a funny anecdote.

"I'll keep mum." His lips hovered close again. Her skin heated and she inhaled deeply, drawing in his masculine scent. Sensation flashed through her as their lips met again.

The kiss was gentle, just their lips touching softly, a goodbye kiss, but it stirred up enough emotion in her heart to frighten the wits out of her. She pulled back. "I really should go."

"If you insist. I'm not sure Melody will be happy to see you." He indicated to their original table with his head.

She turned to see Melody sitting in Bowie's lap. "Oh my goodness. We'd better go rescue him."

"What makes you think it's him that needs rescuing?"

"I know Melody better than you do. And please don't tell her about our kiss, either."

"You're making me feel like your dirty little secret." His gaze swept over her body, stirring a wave of heat. "I think I like that."

Tara blinked. *Uh-oh.* This was already starting to

feel like a bad idea. At least from her brain's perspective. Her body felt very differently. She rose to her feet and hurried across the rooftop garden to the table. "Melody, what are you doing to this poor man?"

Bowie looked up with a wry smile. "She said the chairs were too hard for her."

"Of course she did." Tara lifted a brow. "We've got a big day tomorrow winning Gareth over. And Jesse has kindly offered to invite him to the after party tomorrow night, so it will be a long day, too. We need some sleep."

"Speak for yourself, darling." Her long fingernails clawed at Bowie's stubbled chin.

"I'm serious, Melody." She put her hands on her hips. Sometimes she had to get tough, though it was hard when your assistant was also your best friend.

"Okay, okay." Melody turned to leer at Bowie. "If you could just put your hands under my butt and push me up, sweetie…"

"Melody!" But Bowie was already obliging. Goodness, the West men were trouble in a very delicious package.

Walking down the Las Vegas strip with two drop-dead handsome six-foot-plus cowboys who just happened to be international rodeo stars was good for any girl's ego. Strangers recognized Jesse and Bowie and wished them luck for tomorrow.

"Just think," said Melody, when they reached their hotel. "By tomorrow night one of you will be world champion and the other will be crying into his beer."

"What if someone else wins?" Bowie tipped his hat back.

"Impossible, darling. And I volunteer to comfort

the loser."

Tara pleaded exhaustion and donned her earplugs and eye mask to avoid being asked for a blow-by-blow account of the evening's activities. Melody slept until nearly noon—as usual—so Tara had managed to recover some semblance of her sanity by the time she awoke.

Melody opened one eye and peered at her from across the room. "Did Jesse kiss you?"

Could she lie? She didn't want her nose to grow any bigger. One of her clients was a plastic surgeon and he'd offered her a discount nose job. She'd been a little sensitive about her nose ever since. Still... "No."

"I don't believe you."

Her stomach churned and she could feel her nose growing already. "He kissed me."

"Ha!" She sat up like a zombie rising from the grave, hair sticking in all directions. "I knew it. Did sparks fly?"

"A few. Did you kiss Bowie?" Maybe she could turn the conversation to Melody's favorite subject—herself.

"I tried." She heaved a sigh. "He's slipperier than an eel. I kept getting his gorgeous stubbled cheek instead."

"Maybe he's seeing someone."

"Like I care!"

"Perhaps he cares?"

"Oh, please. These rodeo cowboys are on the road all year and sleep with a different woman in every town. Don't worry, I'll kiss him tonight. I have my ways and means. Unless you want to switch?"

"Switch what?"

"Men of course, darling. Jesse is very easy on the eyes. And frankly he's more likely to win the million dollars. He's the number one seed. Bowie's only number three."

"I don't think they call it seeds in rodeo. I think it's rankings, or something."

"Who cares? As long as one of those handsome young men is sowing their seed inside me tomorrow, they can call it what they want." She winked. "And I'd even marry a cowboy if he had a million dollars in his pocket."

"You are a danger to yourself and others. Jesse plans to spend that money building out some ranch land if he wins it."

"Then I'll stick with Bowie and if he wins he can blow it all on me." She stretched. "Either way, we're both getting laid tonight."

"Melody, stop it! Our number one goal here in Vegas is to get Gareth to sign on the dotted line of our contract. That will pay for the rent on my depressing new apartment and allow me to continue eating food on a regular basis. I don't want you to derail our mission by drooling all over Bowie and forgetting about our client."

"Maybe I should sleep with Gareth. He's loaded."

"No! Don't even entertain such a terrible thought. This is business. I haven't paid nearly enough attention to business over the last few years and I need to fix that right now."

"Nonsense. You need to get laid so you get Gordon out of your mind and move on with your life. You'll be a lot more fun to work with once you learn to relax." She pulled on her satin robe. "In fact, I have a proposition for you."

"No thanks." Jesse's little deal from last night was quite enough.

"You sleep with Jesse, and I *won't* sleep with Gareth."

Tara froze. Melody *was* crazy enough to seduce their client. She might even get him drunk enough to succeed, too, and that would really be a death-knell for the contract when he woke up next to her with a huge hangover. "I thought you wanted Bowie."

Melody sighed and meandered toward the bathroom. "Tragically I don't think he's interested in me. I probably am old enough to be his mother if I had a teen pregnancy. Which thank goodness I didn't."

Tara heard water running and turned back to the spreadsheet of proposed expenses she was preparing for Gareth. Hopefully Melody would forget her little challenge and they could have a reasonably enjoyable and productive day.

They arrived at the arena in plenty of time before the finals, and sat with Gareth and his friends in his VIP box. When Tara told him about the after party, he was almost speechless. "You know Jesse West?"

"We were at school together. In the North East." She smiled sweetly. It did sound rather fabulous. Very designer-to-the-rich-and-famous, which was of course what she aspired to be.

"Well I'll be..." He shook his head and sighed. "You're quite something Ms. Kent. I'd be tickled pink to attend." Melody gave her a surreptitious thumbs up, and they sat down to await the rides.

"I hope you haven't forgotten my offer," said Melody, as they sipped some of their host's champagne.

"I'm not paying any attention to your foolishness." Tara scanned the area where the bulls and the contestants emerged from, but had not so far seen any sign of Jesse or Bowie.

"You should. I only have your best interests at heart." Melody was in high gear today, laughing, talking a mile a minute, and flirting with everyone—including Gareth. "But I'll make it easier on you." She paused to sip her champagne, then leaned in to whisper. "If Jesse *wins*, you'll sleep with him."

"Maybe he doesn't want to."

Melody snorted. "You and I both know that's nonsense. Why are you so resistant? He's gorgeous."

"I'm still fragile. I only broke up with Gordon a few weeks ago and turned my whole life upside down."

"Then set it right side up again. Seriously, if he doesn't win, or he's not interested, then you're off the hook. If he does, and he is—then promise me you'll take advantage of this delicious opportunity."

"What if he just wants revenge sex because I kissed him then disappeared out of his life without a word of goodbye?"

"Enjoy it!"

"But what if I get my heart broken?" she whispered.

"What heart? This is about sex, darling. And seriously, did you see the way Gareth was checking me out? He'd be mine in a heartbeat. In fact he reminds me a little of my second husband, but much, much richer. I think he and I could make some very special magic together."

"I should fire you." She tried to look stern.

"You should, but you won't. You know I bring in the clients."

Tara sighed. "Unfortunately I do."

"Deal?" Melody flashed her eyes, which today were ringed with a lot of expertly applied black eyeliner.

"I must be an idiot for agreeing to anything so stupid, but okay. If he wins—and only if he wins—and if he's really interested, then I'll be... receptive."

A wicked grin spread across Melody's mouth. "Excellent, darling. I knew you'd see sense."

Tara glanced around the arena, and down to the gate where the first bull was ready to run out into the ring. Maybe Jesse wouldn't win. And if he did he'd probably be too busy with fans and buckle bunnies to even remember her. She'd be back in the hotel tonight fine tuning her design and her expense spreadsheet and saying *I told you so* to Melody.

"And first up today we have Bowie West, who—along with his brother Jesse West—has shown impressive stamina and staying power here for the last three years. Today he'll be riding Fiery Biscuit, a yellow bull with a ferocious attitude and a near vertical buck."

Bowie could win. Tara sipped her champagne. Then she'd be off the hook. Bowie wound the leather rope around his hand, settling himself down onto the bull's back. The brim of his cowboy hat hid his face but she bet there were a lot of emotions running through him right now.

The gate opened and the big yellow bull rushed out, and immediately did a handstand on its front legs. She almost spilled her champagne as Bowie lurched forward. He managed to sit back down on the bull as it landed, but when it spun hard to the right he went left. He hit the ground hard then rolled and sprang to his feet. His hat had fallen off and as he walked to pick it up she could see the disappointment on his face.

"Rats." Melody took a big gulp of her champagne. "I bet he'll be bummed about that. He probably won't be in the mood to celebrate tonight."

"I think he'll take it in stride." Tara scanned the area behind the bull pen for Jesse, but it was hard to tell who anyone was since they all wore big cowboy hats that hid their faces from this angle. "Besides, it's not like you to give up easily." She might as well encourage Melody to pursue Bowie, as it would keep her hands off Gareth.

The next two riders stayed on, but neither of them had especially high scores, because their bulls didn't throw enough crazy antics. The fourth one fell off and was hurt, so medics rushed into the arena to treat him and the audience murmured. "These guys really are crazy, aren't they?" Tara would hate to see Jesse sprawled on the dirt like that, wincing in pain. "I'm glad they wear protective vests, but I don't get why most of them don't wear helmets."

"You already said it, sweetie. They're crazy."

"You'd have to be crazy yourself to date someone who did this for a living. Their wives and girlfriends must be so anxious every time they ride."

Melody's brow lifted. "You're worried about Jesse, aren't you?"

"Of course. I would hate for him to get hurt."

"Me too, because I'm really looking forward to hearing about your adventures tonight."

Tara glared at her.

"Look, Jesse's up next." The medics took the injured rider out of the arena—he managed to wave encouragingly at the fans as they carried him out on the stretcher—and Tara's heart twisted into a knot as she watched Jesse—face hidden by his big white hat, but distinctive broad build clearly recognizable beneath a pale checkered shirt and faded denim— wind the rope around his hand.

6

"The next rider is Jesse West." The announcer's voice boomed over the arena. "This is his third year on the circuit. He's held the number one rank since summertime and he'd like to take home the big prize this year. He's riding one of the toughest bulls we have here today, a four year old from Missouri by the name of Radiator Grill."

The gate slid open and Tara gasped as the huge black and white bull took off across the arena bucking. Melody gripped her wrist, digging her long fingernails into the skin, but she barely notice as the bull spun sideways and Jesse's hat went flying. The logos on his leather protective vest were a blur. Surely eight seconds was over by now? She saw daylight between his butt and the saddle and gripped Melody back.

The crowd roared. That was good, right? But Jesse was still getting tossed around by the bull and—

In a flash he leaped off and the bullfighters rushed into coax the bull back into a pen. Jesse picked up his hat then turned to glance up at the scoreboard.

"Fingers crossed, darling. At least a ninety. Ninety three would be nice."

"How do you know?" She turned to stare at

Melody.

"Making conversation with Bowie last night, of course."

"Oh." Tara stared at the scoreboard as the numbers flipped to 92.5. People in the stands around them stood up and roared. "Does this mean he won?"

She wanted him to win—of course, who wouldn't?—on the other hand, Melody could hold onto one of her silly ideas like a pit bull with an old shoe.

"Unless someone scores a 93." Bowie's voice above her made her startle. "Which isn't totally impossible but pretty darn unlikely."

"We're sorry you fell off, darling," said Melody with a sympathetic expression.

"Me too." Bowie shrugged and shone a wry smile. "All in a day's work, though. Cold beer anyone?"

Jesse high-fived some of his buddies on his way up to the stands. Damn. Ninety-two-point-five. That was a winning score, especially with Bowie out of the running.

He turned to watch the next contestant, who hit the dust at the five second mark. Four more to go.

Tara was up in the VIP enclosure. He'd seen the worried look on her face right before his ride, and he liked it. That look meant she cared.

And the kisses they'd shared last night…. He let out a rush of air as heat flooded his body. He really shouldn't rush into anything with Tara, though. He needed to take it slow and steady, treat her like the lady she'd always been, and woo her like a gentleman.

Because he'd like to spend a lot of time with Tara.

"Oh Lord, I hope you're retiring, Jesse." An older

man who trained one of his rivals shook his hand.

"That's the plan."

"Glad to hear it. I've half a mind to have the officials check your jeans for Velcro."

"You know good balance when you see it, J.D."

"I sure do." He gave Jesse a hug. "Don't spend that whole million on your first night out, okay?"

"I have to win it first."

J.D. winked. They both knew he was pretty much a shoe-in to win it, but it would be tacky to crow over a victory before his name was announced. And someone else could still score higher and win today's event.

The next rider stayed on but the score wasn't even ninety. He could see Bowie talking with Tara and Melody. Would she give him a kiss again? He could argue that he deserved it after that ride.

Another rider had scored a 91 by the time he got to the stairs. Close but no cigar.

After the last rider parted ways with his bull, the announcer declared Jesse the winner and the crowd roared. He entered the VIP enclosure, glad-handing everyone in sight, and headed for Tara.

"Congratulations." Her smile did something crazy to his heart.

"Thanks for bringing me luck." He leaned in for a kiss, hope beating in his veins.

She deftly offered a soft cheek, and he took what he could get. They had an entire night ahead of them.

Bowie hugged him. "You deserve it, bro. And now, with you out of the way, I'll finally get to win some buckles again."

"It's your own fault for dragging me into bull riding. I was quite happy riding horses until you got lonely on the circuit."

"Now I'll be on my own again." Bowie looked rueful.

"Not for long, I'll bet, cowboy," cut in Melody, with a wink. They all laughed softly, but it was a bittersweet moment. Hopefully Bowie would get the jones to settle down soon, too, whether he won the title or not. The bull riding game was fun for a young guy, but sooner or later you had to call it quits or a bull would do it for you.

"Don't you have someone to introduce me too?" Jesse looked curiously at Tara. He wanted to go all out fulfilling his end of the bargain. Then maybe he could go back for a second helping.

"Oh, yes, where's Gareth?" She acted like she'd forgotten all about it. Of course it probably wasn't ladylike to make bargains over kisses and she was every inch a lady. She looked like a cool drink of lemonade today in sexy faded jeans and a pale yellow shirt with white embroidery. "Let me go get him."

"I'll come too." He didn't want to risk losing her. And the view from back here was quite something.

"Gareth!" She called to a guy in his early fifties, wearing a gaudy black and white shirt and a big black hat. "There's someone I'd like you to meet."

Gareth's face glowed as Jesse shook his hand and shared a few comments about his ride. "And I do hope you'll join me as my guest at tonight's party."

"I'd be very pleased to." Gareth looked fondly at Tara. "Tara's quite a girl. I bet she was sharp as a tack back when you were in school together."

"She certainly was." Jesse noticed a teeny blush creeping over her cheeks. "I bet she'll do an amazing job designing your house."

"If he hires me," protested Tara.

"Why wouldn't he? You're the best."

"Has she done work for you?" Gareth looked very interested.

"We've been making plans to decorate the ranch I'm moving to when I quit the circuit. She's going to do all the designs." The white lie rolled off his tongue. And why not? He'd never seen her designs but she was one of those people who were good at everything. He'd be happy to hire her.

If he needed to. Maybe they'd be an item by then and she'd be decorating her own house.

The thought rushed his brain, crowding out all others, and causing him to miss the next couple of exchanges in the conversation.

"Don't you think, Jesse?" Tara looked at him expectantly.

"Oh, yes," he agreed, with no clue what he'd just said yes to. The prospect of Tara in his life—in his bed—had scattered his thoughts like arena dust under the feet of a bull. "Why don't we all head to the party and get some dinner?"

Tara couldn't believe how well this was going. The party was a *Who's Who* of rodeo stars from past and present, all gathered in a luxurious ballroom at one of the ritziest hotels on the strip. Food and drink flowed freely, and her client was enjoying the time of his life.

As the party wore on, Gareth started discussing little details of the project—the stone fountain to be imported from Tuscany, the frescoes they'd commission from a local artist—as if it were already a work in progress. She could practically feel those sweet greenbacks flowing into her empty bank account.

Jesse was the man of the hour and everyone wanted to slap him on the back and share a drink with him. Several times she tried to discreetly slip away. She didn't want him to feel like he was stuck obeying the high school edict to, "leave with the girl you brought," when so many more glittering opportunities presented themselves to him by the minute.

But minutes, if not seconds later, he stood right there beside her again. "I'm starting to think we should bust out of here," he whispered.

"Can you do that? You're the star."

"I can do anything I like. I'm retired now. Picked up my prize money and everything."

"How do they give you the million dollars? Is it in a big suitcase?" He probably had a huge check in his back pocket. Or maybe on the floor somewhere. People did say she was neurotic, but still, best to ask…

"Yeah. I left it in the coat check." He smiled warmly. "I hope it's okay."

She stared. He was kidding, right? He always had been rather too kind and trusting. Her heart started pounding. She'd warned him in the past not to always assume the best of people.

"I authorized an electronic transfer into my bank account." His smile creased into a grin. "I did have you going there."

"Nothing surprises me anymore. At least if it's in the bank you can't spend it all tonight buying people drinks."

"I'm not that kind of cowboy. I have serious plans. And I need to save most of it for when you decorate my ranch."

She glanced over her shoulder to make sure Gareth wasn't nearby. "I can't believe you said that."

"Don't make me a liar." He leaned in, and for a hot panicky second she thought he was going to kiss her right here in front of everyone. But he apparently thought better of it. "C'mon. Let's go."

"What about Melody?" She hadn't seen her friend in a solid half-hour. And the last time she did see her she was laughing with Gareth.

"I asked Bowie to make sure she gets home safely."

"Are you sure he won't forget? There's a lot of temptation here tonight."

He winked, and that adorable grin made dimples in his cheeks. "I trust him like a brother."

Even out on the street, total strangers recognized Jesse and whooped and hollered at him. He took it all in stride, and graciously signed several autographs. They'd walked a full block before she finally had the courage to ask, "Where are we going?"

"That's a good question. I just wanted to get you to myself. How about we go back to my hotel? I have a suite, so there's a nice sitting room with a full stocked bar and some really good champagne on ice."

Gulp. His hotel room? Her breath quickened. Still, if she went there, she could at least insinuate to Melody that she and Jesse had— "What do cowboys know about really good champagne?"

"I guess you'd better come find out."

7

The elevator took them to the top floor of the hotel, and as soon as the door opened she could tell this was not your average suite. The walked into an elegant living room the size of her entire apartment, with a wall of glass that provided a breathtaking view over Las Vegas.

No big deal. Most of her clients were this rich. Gordon probably was too, though he'd never revealed more than a tantalizing hint about his net worth. "So, let's see this champagne?" Probably a fifty-dollar bottle of Moët.

"I admit, I don't know much about champagne. My buddy Armand sent this to me yesterday. He owns a little vineyard in France."

"So it's his local homebrew?"

"Pretty much."

She looked at the label. Krug, Clos D'Ambonnay 2002. She blinked. Jesse might not know too much about champagne, but she'd taken a course. "This champagne is worth about two thousand dollars a bottle."

"It better be good, then." He put his hat down on the table and started to tear off the foil.

"Are you sure you don't want to save it for a

special occasion?"

"This is a special occasion." He peeled back the wire.

She laughed. "I guess you did just win the World Finals."

"Forget about that." His eyes sparkled. "The woman of my dreams—the one that got away—is right here with me in my hotel room. It doesn't get any better than that."

"I'm glad we ran into each other." She meant it. Her heart felt pretty full right now. It was sweet of him to share this special night with her, and treat her like a queen, after the way she'd deserted him all those years ago.

He poured the champagne into two tall flutes and handed one to her. "To the future."

"The future." The toast was nice and innocuous and didn't imply any particular kind of future. She drank a sparkly sip. The full, rich flavor took a couple of seconds to spread over her tongue. "Oh my goodness. This is very good champagne."

"You deserve the best."

"I'm not at all sure what I deserve, but it was very kind of you to help me win over my client today. You went above and beyond."

"I had powerful motivation." His dark gaze rested on her face for a moment, and the expression in his eyes made her breath catch. "I wanted to be important to you."

"You already were important to me. You were one of my closest friends." Until that kiss.

"In another life that you left without a second glance. I didn't want to be just some old flame who reminds you of a time you'd rather forget. I want to mean something to you right here and right now."

He put his champagne glass down on the polished wood bar and slid his arms around her waist. Heat flared low in her belly. The champagne buzzed in her brain and her nipples tightened in awareness of his hard body.

"You've changed a lot." She breathed the words as he gathered her closer, then took her champagne flute from her hand. "You're a lot bolder."

Now his mouth hovered only inches from hers and her lips quivered in anticipation.

"If you want something in life you have to go after it with all guns blazing." His low voice crept into her ears. "And I want you."

His words struck a primal chord deep inside her.

I want you, too.

Their lips met and a hot flash of desire swept through her as his tongue plunged into her mouth. His hard chest crushed her breasts with delicious force and her hips pressed hard against his sturdy thighs. His strong body and take-no-prisoners attitude turned her on more than was decent and reasonable.

She'd never been aroused like this. Her insides throbbed, aching for him. What was happening to her? She'd dated Gordon for at least three months before the prospect of sex was even broached.

But with Jesse, she wanted it right here, right now, and her panties might catch fire if it didn't happen soon.

His big hand cupped her butt, a gesture so bold and primal that it shocked her and turned her on at the same time. She shoved her fingers into his thick hair, and enjoyed the hard ledge of his cheekbones. Then she let her hands roam lower to explore the thick muscle of his back through his shirt, then lower to the firm backside encased by his jeans.

Her breathing came harder and faster even though they still stood in his hotel living room, fully clothed. She opened her eyes to peek and see if she was imagining the whole thing. "There aren't any curtains on the windows."

"We're a hundred feet over the city. No one can see in."

"But airplanes…" He silenced her with a hot and steady kiss that stole her senses and crumbled her inhibitions. She reached into his jeans, past the thick leather belt, to un-tuck his shirt and press her fingers into his hot skin.

"We'll have more privacy in the bedroom." His voice was a rasped whisper.

The bedroom. That meant only one thing—and it wasn't sleep. "Yes."

He grabbed her hand—as if she might try to run—and tugged her gently through a doorway into a luxurious bedroom with soft white bedding turned down and ready.

His big fingers fumbled with the buttons on her delicate pale yellow shirt, so she moved in to help him. While she undid the buttons, he unzipped her jeans and slid them down over her thighs with a sigh. "I need to take your boots off." He looked up at her from down by her hips, eyes glowing with desire. "You'd better sit down."

She managed to maneuver herself onto the bed, which was awkward with her jeans pushed down and her shirt half off. How did she forget about her boots? He pulled them off one by one and tossed them behind him, then pulled her jeans the rest of the way off. Now she wore only her bra—a lacy pale yellow one that coordinated with her shirt—and matching panties.

"Oh my." Jesse shook his head, taking in the view of her barely-clad body as if she were the first watering hole after a six-day roundup in the desert. "I'll admit that I dreamed of this moment, but I never imagined it would be as good as this."

"You have too many clothes on," she protested. She finished un-tucking his shirt and unbuttoned it with feverish haste. He'd already unzipped his jeans and kicked off his boots and they pushed the denim down over his powerful thighs together.

He wore dark grey underwear that did absolutely nothing to conceal his impressive erection.

Tara wanted to smile. Jesse was every bit as aroused as her. That made her feel desirable—beautiful, even—for the first time in quite a while.

His body was unbelievable. Thick hard muscle with a sprinkling of dark hair leading down below the waistband of his shorts. She traced the trail with her fingertip and watched his skin flinch under her touch. He inhaled sharply as she touched the hard flesh, which jumped in response. His arousal was so intense she could almost feel it in the air, and sparks jumped between them.

She wanted him inside her. Easing her fingertips into the waistband of his underwear, she tugged it slowly down, and watched as he sprang free.

"Now you're wearing too many clothes," he growled softly. He tried to unhook her bra, but kept getting distracted by kissing her, so she finally helped him out. He caressed each of her nipples with his hot mouth, then he pulled her undies gently down over her legs. Eyes glazed with passion, he surveyed her from head to toe. "Much better."

He helped her into position up on the soft bed, and rolled on the condom. Her belly quivered with anticipation as he climbed over her, all six-foot-whatever of big, bull riding male.

He entered her with exquisite tenderness, kissing her softly on the lips, sinking gently inside her while she opened up for him. *Oh Jesse.* Her arms tightened around him, pulling him closer.

I need you. Her life had been a long, hard ride lately and it felt so good to relax into his sturdy, masculine embrace and let him take her away.

Emotion built inside her as she remembered the hopes and dreams she'd shared with him all those years ago, buried under the pile of small joys and large disappointments of the years in between—especially the crushing end of her long engagement. That wasn't an engagement at all.

She felt her heart beat faster and harder, and it started to spread its wings and rise again, like a phoenix from the ashes, as Jesse breathed life and fire back into her.

Passion and sensation build inside her as Jesse thrust into her. She heard her voice cry out his name, then a shout of passion as a climax swept over her with stunning force. For an instant she felt like she was all alone, floating out in the universe, surrounded by blackness and distant stars, then she felt Jesse's warm, caring arms around her, drawing her back down to earth.

"Are you all right, Tara?" His warm, masculine voice soothed her.

"I'm more than all right." She blinked, trying to

make out his familiar face in the dim light of the bedroom while silver stars still danced in her vision. She'd never had an orgasm like that before. "I don't think I've ever been better."

"I'm glad to hear it." He kissed her cheek. "This is a dream come true, for me. You have no idea how many adolescent nights I spent wondering what it would feel like to hold you in my arms."

"I'm glad I didn't. I suspect it would have scared me off. I was really shocked at myself for kissing you."

"It was right before the summer vacation. Maybe you knew you weren't coming back?"

"Maybe." Perhaps she had known, in some weird, unconscious way, that night would be her last chance to kiss him.

Until now.

"If you hadn't kissed me, would you have stayed in touch?"

"No," she admitted. "I deliberately lost touch with everyone. That's one reason I changed my name. I didn't want people looking me up on social media and asking what happened."

"It wasn't your fault."

"No, but I was devastated and ashamed all the same. Everyone thought I was so perfect, and that I was going to get straight A's and get into Princeton, then have a big career..." her voice drifted off. "I didn't even get good grades my senior year. I felt like a fish out of water at a huge public high school and I lost my confidence. I'm not sure I ever got it back."

"Then it's about time you did." He stroked her cheek with his thumb.

"How?"

"Doing all the things you always wanted to."

"Princeton tuition is still rather out of my reach."

He laughed, which created those adorable creases around his eyes. "Not Princeton. That would take you too far away. And those New England winters...." He pretended to shiver. "But it looks like you clinched your big commission, so that can be the beginning of a big new upswing."

"I certainly hope so. If all goes well I can convince Gareth to let one of the prestigious publications, like *Vogue* or *Architectural Digest* photograph it. Then more big-money clients will seek me out."

"You will still find the time to decorate my ranch, though?" He lifted a brow.

She laughed. "You're funny. And sweet. Where is it?"

"It's in the hill country, of course. Not too far from Austin. Right now it's a ramshackle collection of old farm buildings and some scraggly fields, but I'm going to call it Singing Pines. I plan to bring in horses that need re-training and make it a nice place people can come for a getaway vacation."

"It doesn't sound like you're quite ready for an interior decorator."

"You should know me better than that by now, Tara. You saw me ride Radiator Grill today. I'm ready for anything."

She rested her head on his broad shoulder. Stray sparkles of heat and desire still danced through her. "You are, aren't you? Hopefully some of that will rub off on me."

"I'd be happy to help." He shifted just enough to jostle their bodies against each other.

She giggled. "Don't be too literal. I'm not naturally

a risk taker."

"Maybe you should be. Everything's a little scary the first time. But if you're brave enough to try it, there's a second time—and in my experience that's even better."

THE END

Read more about the West brothers in the forthcoming books in the **Hearts of the West** series. Jesse and Tara's story continues in **His Untamed Heart: The Cowboy's Christmas Reunion**.

Learn more and join the new release mailing list at www.jenlewis.com.

ABOUT THE AUTHOR

Jennifer Lewis loves heat in all its forms including spicy food, steamy temperatures and smoking hot heroes. She is a USA TODAY bestselling author and her books have been translated into more than twenty languages. She lives in sunny South Florida and when she's not sitting at her laptop she can often be found at the beach. Read more about her books and join her new release mailing list at www.jenlewis.com.